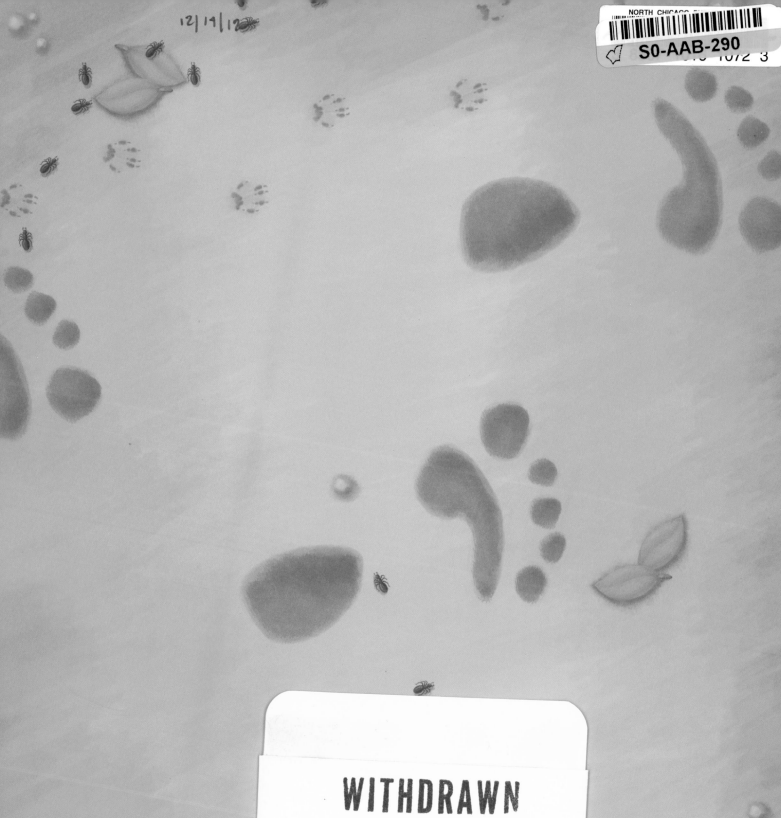

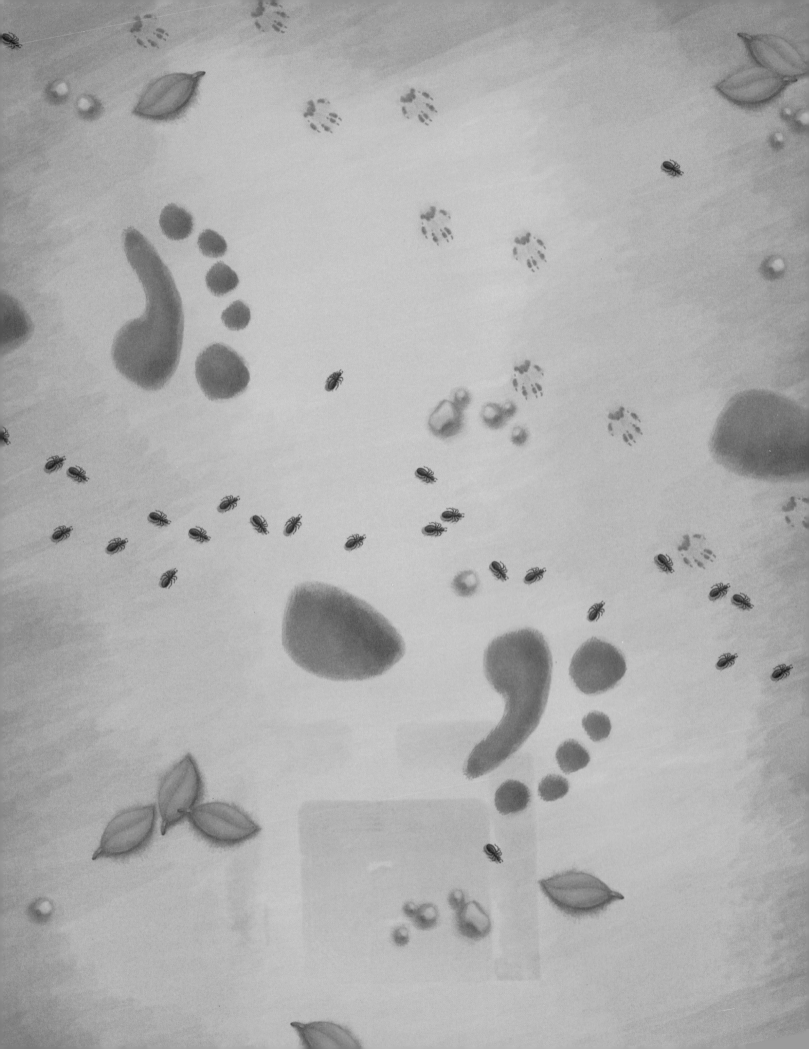

MR. BIGGS
at the Circus
El Sr. Grande en el circo

written and illustrated by
escrito e ilustrado por

Kevin Bloomfield

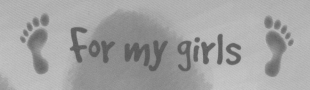

For my girls

Bloomfield, Kevin.

Mr. Biggs at the Circus / written and illustrated by Kevin Bloomfield; translated by Cambridge BrickHouse = El Sr. Grande en el circo / escrito e ilustrado por Kevin Bloomfield; traducción al español de Cambridge BrickHouse —1 ed. — McHenry, IL ; Raven Tree Press, 2012.

p. ; cm.

SUMMARY: Will Mr. Biggs find out that he fits at the circus… or is he too big?

Bilingual Edition
ISBN 978-1-936299-98-0 hardcover

English Edition
ISBN 978-1-936299-99-7 hardcover

Audience: pre-K to 3rd grade.
Title available in bilingual English-Spanish or English-only editions.

1. Humorous Stories — Juvenile fiction. 2. Circus — Juvenile fiction. 3. Folklore — Juvenile fiction. 4. Bilingual books—English and Spanish. 5. [Spanish language materials-books.] I. Illust. Bloomfield, Kevin. II. Title. III. El Sr. Grande en el circo

Library of Congress Control Number: 2011921187

Printed in Taiwan
10 9 8 7 6 5 4 3 2 1
First Edition

Free activities for this book are available at www.raventreepress.com

Mr. Biggs is a sasquatch, also known as bigfoot.

El señor Grande es un simio gigante. Algunos lo llaman Pie Grande.

3

Mr. Biggs loves
to hike near the creek.

Al Sr. Grande le
encanta ir de excursión
cerca del arroyo.

4

He stops to read
a colorful sign.

Se detiene para leer
Un colorido cartel.

5

The circus is full of many amazing things.
It looks like fun!

El circo está lleno de mil cosas asombrosas.
¡Parece DIVERTIDO!

Mr. Biggs wants to join the circus.

El Sr. Grande quiere unirse al circo.

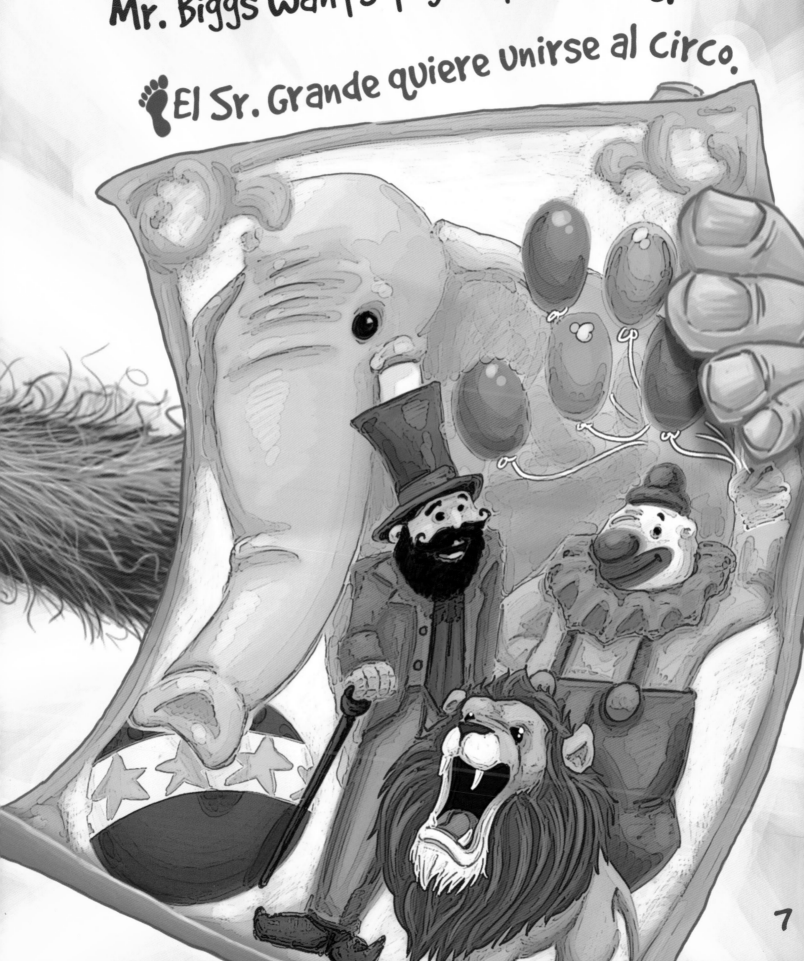

7

Mr. Biggs jumps over the creek, crawls under the bridge and runs down the mountain

El Sr. Grande salta por encima del arroyo, se arrastra por debajo del puente y baja por la montaña

8

to the big circus tent.
He sneaks inside.
He wants to be in the circus.

hacia la gran carpa del circo.
Él se cuela dentro.
¡Quiere estar en el circo!

9

Mr. Biggs meets the clowns.

El Sr. Grande conoce a los payasos.

10

Juggling hurts his head.

El malabarismo le da dolor de cabeza.

He won't do that again.

No lo intentará de nuevo.

11

Mr. Biggs tries the human cannon.
"BOOOOOM!"

El Sr. Grande intenta el número del cañón humano.
¡PRACATÁN!

That didn't work.

Eso no funcionó.

14

Mr. Biggs spots some **HUGE** animals.

El Sr. Grande descubre algunos animales **ENORMES**.

18

Mr. Biggs thinks the bearded lady is cute.

El Sr. Grande piensa que la mujer barbuda es linda.

Long beards are very itchy.

Las barbas largas dan picazón.

He should know.

Él debe saberlo bien.

The bear is a very good dancer.

La osa es una bailarina muy buena.

Mr. Biggs likes dancing with the bear.
They prefer Salsa!

Al Sr. Grande le gusta bailar con ella.
¡Ellos prefieren Salsa!

Mr. Biggs tries the trapeze.

El Sr. Grande intenta el trapecio.

The lions and tigers roar very loudly.

Los leones y tigres rugen muy alto.

26

Mr. Biggs tries fire dancing.

El Sr. Grande intenta la la danza del fuego.

28

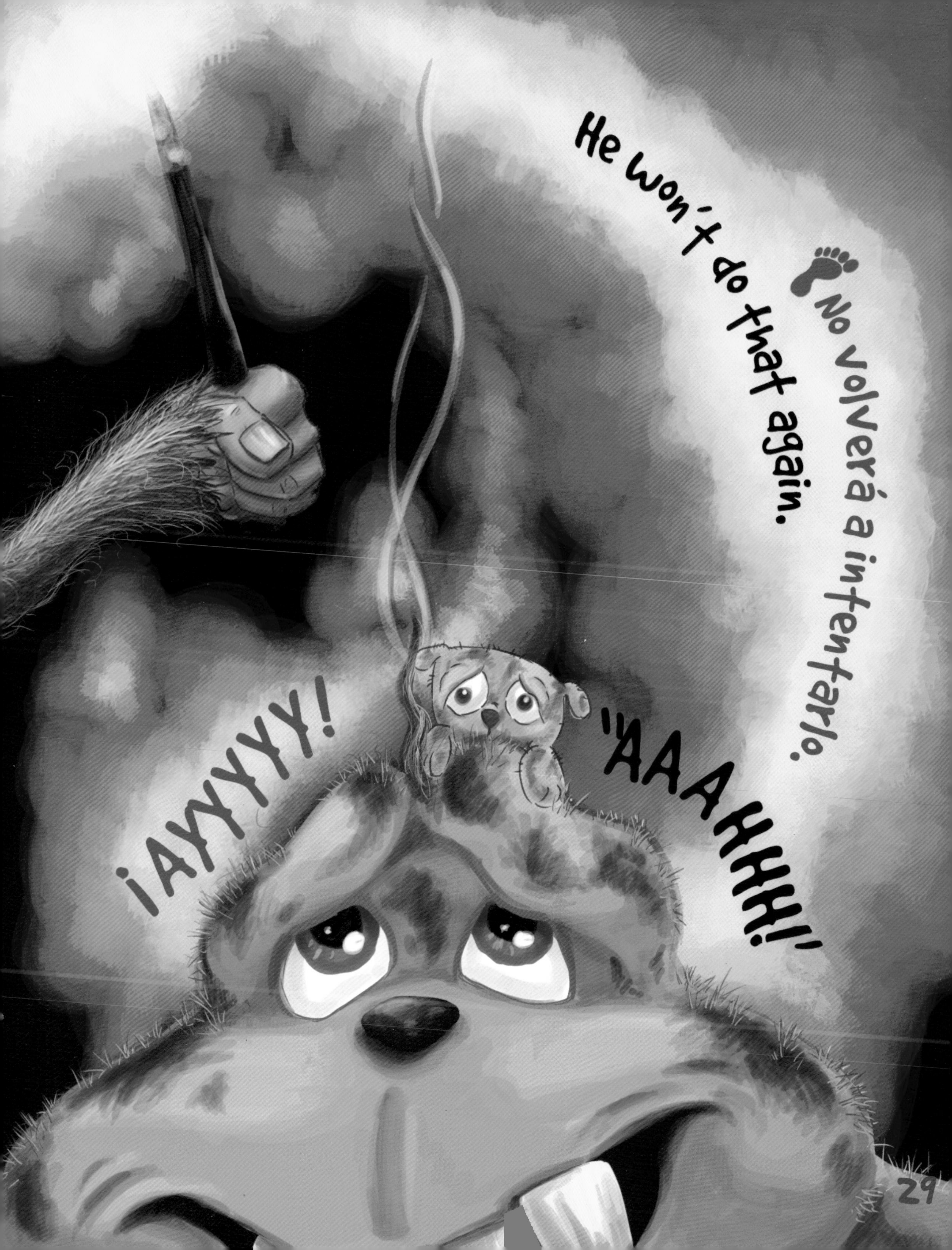
He won't do that again.
No volverá a intentarlo.
¡AYYYY!
"AAAHHH!"

The Children cheer
as he lifts the entire circus.
Mr. Biggs loves the circus!

Los niños lo aplauden
mientras él levanta
el circo entero.
¡Al Sr. Grande le
encanta
el circo!

30

Mr. Biggs loves to lift heavy things.

Al Sr. Grande le gusta levantar cosas pesadas.

Vocabulary   Vocabulario

English	Español
hike	excursión
creek	arroyo
sign	cartel
circus	circo
bridge	puente
mountain	montaña
clown	payaso
cannon	cañón
animal(s)	animales
bearded lady	mujer barbuda
dancer	bailarina
dizzy	marean
roar	rugen
fire	fuego
lift	levantar
heavy	pesadas
cheer	aplauden